Life- A Blooming Bud

Author

Debalina Sarkar

Publisher

Power In Me Foundation

ISBN: 978-81-954847-6-8

Book Name

Life- A Blooming Bud (Paperback)

Author: Debalina Sarkar

Copyright

The author holds all the copyright of the content as it is her original work and has granted the rights to publish and distribute to Publisher- Power In Me Foundation in all its formats.

ISBN: 978-81-954847-6-8

Copyright reserved @ 2021

Publisher

POWER IN ME FOUNDATION

H.No. 531, MIG-21, Opp. SBI Colony, Ganiyari Road, Waidhan, District-Singrauli, Madhya Pradesh, Pin Code-4863886, Email : mpowerinme@gmail.com

Printer

Waidhan, Singrauli, Madhya Pradesh
Pin code- 486886

Foreward

Words have power stored in them. They can fuel your imagination and heal you from your traumas. Often in the form of poetries and stories we experience that magic of words. This book Life- A Blooming Bud is a wonderful journey from Debalina Sarkar. I call it a journey because as you start you will move to your childhood when you loved to hear the stories from your grand parents and let your imagination loose. Grand Ma's Gopal is a perfect start to the book. What I most love about this book is that it has poems and stories that are easy to understand. Children would love to read those lovely stories like Toothy the tooth fairy. A sense of adventure and life lessons to keep in mind. One chapter or a story on the perspective about friendship from a dog's point of view is a great take and you fall in love. If you are young adult, you will enjoy the love story about lovers. We can even read poems about selflove and woman empowerment. A classy story how right environment is sufficient to allow talent to bloom. The book has beautifully handled some of the tough emotions and interactions among relationships. When you read the story about the Grand father and his granddaughter, the emotions overwhelm. The author has beautifully put it together. We can even see some spirituality in the poems and small prose to enjoy. Overall, the book is a great read from child to youth to old age. Everyone can read and enjoy.

Manoj Kumar Singh, Life Coach, Researcher, Publisher, Author, Motivational Speaker, Poet, Podcaster, Social Entrepreneur and Mentor.
LinkedIn: manojksingh1
Instagram: manojkumarsingh_dilse

Preface

'Life - A Blooming Bud' represents life. Life being a journey-no two days are same. There are days which are packed and one becomes too tired at the end of the day. In such a situation the poetry would be a perfect read. On the days when one is free and has the time to relax, sipping a cup of hot coffee, the stories in the book can be a great companion. This book is a conglomeration of my different writings, which includes both stories and poems as well. This book represents the different experiences and adventures of one during different stages of his or her life. The book contains stories and poetry written for all age groups; children, adolescents, adults and elderly people. The book also caters to people of different tastes. This book provides prose for the prose lovers along with an opportunity to enjoy poetry and vise-versa. The illustrations in the book not only would provide happiness to the young readers but also to others within whom the little child still feels excited and happy to look at the pictures side by side as they read through the book. I tried my best to cover the entire life cycle, the journey of a human being through different phases. Can be considered assorted writings within a single cover. Enjoy reading!

Acknowledgement

'Life - A Blooming Bud' is my first solo book written with lots of love in the heart. For this I would like to thank my parents who encouraged me to write. A special thanks to Mr. Sourav Bhattacharjee for taking out time to edit all my stories and poems and suggesting changes. And thank you Mr. Manoj Kumar Singh, the founder of Ruh-E-Mohabbat for giving me this opportunity to publish my own book. Last but not the least, I thank all my readers for your love.

Content

1. Grandma's Gopal

"Good morning Vrij' wished Vrij's mother as she pulled back the curtain of his room allowing the sunrays to come in. "Mom, please a little later it's Sunday." said Vrij as he pulled up the blanket on top of his face. "Well, okay, you can sleep. I came to tell you Pu woke up and is about to have the tasty laddus that grandpa had bought yesterday for breakfast" said his mother quietly near his covered ears. Immediately Vrij jumped up and rushed to the bathroom after throwing his blanket aside.

Vrij is a 6 year old boy. He had grown up looking at his grandma's 'Gopal'. Since he was a baby, he had seen his grandma worshipping Gopal every day and feeding him like a baby with all sorts of sweets, chocolates and other delicacies meant for the Gods and the kids. When Vrij was a baby, he had extreme curiosity towards that idol of Gopal. He could not pronounce the name Gopal, his grandma taught him he can call him 'Gopu' for short but with time Gopu turned 'Pu' which was more convenient for littleVrij to pronounce. His mom sometimes contemplates the time when Vrij was just a baby of 3 years and he used to crawl up towardsGopal and used to bring him down from his altar and play with him as if one of his dolls. Vrij used to make him sit in his car toys and give him a ride and sometimes when he was tired, he used to sleep hugging Gopal on the mattress. His mom scolded him many times but his grandma was always happy to see them together. She often used to say "we all worship the lord by keeping him at the altar, but how many of us can really make him a friend and play with him."

Vrij is now 6 years old and his fascination for Gopal has not relinquished. He still treats him and talks to him as a friend and expects his Pu would not eat anything without giving Vrij his share. Vrij ran hurriedly towards the puja room. His grandma was sitting and making the garland of flowers. He saw in front a plate of laddus kept near the lord along with some other sweets. Vrij sighed an air of relief. He had seen those yesterday and since then he wanted to taste them at least once. Last night before his 'Pu' slept, Vrij had come and told him "Pu grandpa had bought those ghee fried laddus. They smell and taste amazing but don't eat them all alone, do wait for me." But this morning when his mom told him that Pu was ready for breakfast, he was extremely disappointed and while he was in the washroom he decided if Pu started eating without him, he would not share his favourite chips with him and none can say anything to him about that. Usually,Gopal's are not supposed to eat anything except sweets but Vrij thought how bored he would be if he had to eat the same types of foods everyday. So, whenever his father gets him chips, popcorn and other savory snacks. he stealthily enters the puja room and gives some of the chips to Pu before he takes a bite then after he finishes eating his share, he takes and eats Pu's share too, considering he had already eaten that.

Looking at his interest towards Gopal, his grandmother often told him stories about Gopal. How he was born, how he was loved by all in Vrindavan, how he used to steal butter and milk pudding and how he grew up and helped and counselled Arjuna in 'Kurukshetra', the battlefield of 'Mahabharata', the famous Indian epic.

"But Thammi, Pu was a boy of 14 when he advised Arjuna. What will I do when I am 14?" asked Vrij while munching on a sweet. "You will be in class 8 dear. Perhaps when you are 14 you can look for a war andfind Arjuna to lend your advice" replied grandmother gleefully. On hearing that Vrij frowned at Gopal, his 'Pu'."I will always give thebest advice" you will see.

Years passed by playing and laughing together. Vrij is now 18 years old and yes, he did not go and fight a war at 14 but he qualified both 10 and 12 with flying colors. Over the years his love for his 'Pu' did not lessen but his way of expressing has become more suppressed and hidden. Vrij now no longer visits pu with chips but silently offers anything he eats to him. He no longer plays with him but always comes to meet him twice a day. He also does not use the name 'Pu' in front of others, he had learnt to pronounce the word 'Gopal' and addresses him using that name. When he completed his 12th, he got the opportunity to study management in Symbiosis College at Pune. Everyone was happy and sad to let him go. It was after 2 weeks of his departure, one day when his mother came to his room to clean it, she found a letter tucked inside one of his jeanspockets. Vrij wrote,

(My Dear Pu,

I will have to go to study further like grandma said you left Vrindavan to do your duty. But unlike you, I will come back soon. Now till the time am not there I give you the responsibility to look after everyone here. And yes, I am leaving back my piggy bank savings which you can use to buy chocolates and all that you like. But why shall I give it to you so easily?? It's your money now, so find it yourself. See you soon Pu. I will visit again during my semester break. Do take care of yourself too. Will miss you a lot, love you. Bye.

Always Yours,

Vrij)

Smile spread across Mrs. Chatterjee's face. She was extremely delighted to her son's letter and prayed to Gopal to take care of him. And while cleaning further, she found an envelope with 5000 rupees in them and it was written on top, 'FIND IT IF YOU CAN'.

2.The Old Moon Lady

Amidst the fluffy clouds of the sky,

There shines a round plate like celestial ball so high.

There in it lives an old woman with strings!

Who spins the yarn and loud she sings.

She, with her fishing hook,

Collects the stars from the corner and nook.

Then she spurns them into a pretty dress,

And delivers them to every address.

6

In every house where lies a baby- newly born,

That sleeps in the cradle and yawns.

In the nursery she quietly walks,

In a lovely voice she sweetly talks.

Taking them in her protective arm,

Blesses them with the star dress charm.

The invisible star dress hugs the child,

Forever protecting from the evil and wild.

3.TOOTHY

Miko kept his fallen tooth under his pillow. He was eight years old and it was his first milk tooth that had fallen. His mom had told him stories about how the tooth fairy visits every child whose milk tooth falls. She collects the fallen tooth from them and gifts them perfectly shaped milky white strong teeth. Miko was very excited about his new milky white teeth.

"Mom, where can I find the fairy? Where does she stay?" asked Miko as he was gulping a huge spoon of vanilla ice-cream to calm down the pain of his swollen gum.

"Well, I don't know Miko, she is busy and will perhaps visit you when she is free" said his mom while cooking. Since then, Miko has been carefully carrying with him his tooth.

In school, he was lost in the thoughts of where to find a tooth fairy. "Perhaps she could be found in the forest", thought Miko. But he will not be allowed to go there alone and he doesn't even know the way.

"Pay attention to your lesson Miko", said his class teacher, rounding her eyes. Miko looked towards his book but his mind travelled in search of the place where the tooth fairy lived.

After the bell rang for tiffin, the children rushed out of the class. Miko sat in the classroom and kept staring at the sky. He was fascinated by the various and intriguing shapes the clouds made in the sky. Some looked like ship, some like Santa Clause, and some like the castle of the prince. "What if the tooth fairy lives in a hut or castle in the forest?" thought Miko, but the problem remains the same, how to get there.

After the lunch break it was the English class. The teacher was giving a reference to a story where a lost child uses his intel ligence and takes lift from the stranger to reach the police station from where he could contact his parents and reach home safely. This story triggered a plan in Miko's head. Earlier he had seen many trucks standing in the markets and asked his mother.

She had told him that they were delivering goods from the main city to their markets.

"So do they come everyday mom?" asked Miko. "No, but whenever there is a need they bring the goods", replied his mom, who was struggling to hold her grocery bags.

"So if those trucks come from the city to deliver goods, perhaps they return again. I can make use of this opportunity to reach the forest on the way to the city", thought Miko. "But what shall I tell mom? She will never allow me to go there."

That day Miko returned home without further thought about how he would take an attempt to sneak out and reach the forest. He returned home and looked at his fallen white baby tooth carefully kept inside a plastic zip pouch. "I will surely get a new tooth in exchange for you", thought Miko with a smile.

Next day he woke up early and gathered some candies in his bag and placed the plastic zip pouch consisting of the fallen tooth inside his pencil case. He thought of a plan to sneak out after school. Instead of getting into the school bus he would quietly move out of the bus line and run to the market. He was scared but the thought of meeting the tooth fairy took away his fear.

After school, Miko sneaked out exactly the way he had planned and reached the market. He found two trucks parked outside the grocery shops. "Uncle, are you going back to the city after you deliver the goods here?" asked Miko politely. "Yes", was the reply from the driver.

Miko planned to do exactly as he had thought before. He pretended to walk away from the truck and hid behind the shop.

After unloading of the goods were done he quietly sneaked inside the back of the truck and hid behind the empty cartoons.

The truck started for the city. The fast movement of the truck made Miko topple over multiple times till he decided that it's a better idea to sit down rather than to stand. Miko was extremely excited as he got a glimpse of the forest on both sides and by this time, he had completely overcome the fear of being lost or scolded by his mother. After reaching the city check post, the truck stood for a moment. Miko thought it was the right time to climb down the truck. He climbed down and entered the forest.

It was like a land of wonders where Miko expected to find his desired tooth fairy and a good replacement of his fallen tooth. Miko walked through the forest looking for sound and every imaginary sign that might indicate the house of the tooth fairy. He has heard a lot of stories about fairies living under the mushroom plant but in reality Miko found the mushroom plant to be too small to serve as a house for anyone. However, he kept on walking and spotted many colourful birds, insects and plants, the names of which he did not know. "I am the new Miko in my wonderland", thought Miko in his mind. He considered himself lucky to have bought the instacam with him which his mother gifted him last birthday. He couldn't find a proper use of it till now. He clicked many pictures as he was walking inside the forest, but suddenly the rain clouds hovered over his head and it started to rain heavily. Miko took shelter under the huge tree and carefully wrapped his camera in a bubble wrap and kept it inside his bag. Then he snuggled under the bush growing under the tree. It was difficult for him to keep dry as the showers were hitting him from all sides even though the tree was big enough to keep him semi dry from above.

"Need some help little Mister?" spoke a voice from behind. Miko looked back and saw a little girl standing followed by two rabbits. She was wearing a bluish white gown, she had her hair open but she was not soaked in rain. Even though it was raining heavily. "Who are you?" asked Miko, looking amazed. "Hello, I am Toothy, the tooth fairy. I guess you came looking for me?" said the girl with a smile.

Miko tried to peek behind her and said "But you do not have wings, my mom told me fairies have wings". Toothy smiled and said, "Yes we all have wings but they are invisible you see and we use them when we want." "Yes but why don't you have it visible like we see in story books?" asked Miko with a curious look in his eyes. "Well you see it's very difficult to move around with such heavy wings being visible, it always gets stuck against the plants and bushes and hinders free movement. And also, if we use it too much, there is a hassle of cleaning and drying them afterwards. So… anyways tell me why you are looking for me?" asked Toothy as she sat on the rock under the tree. "Well, I lost one milk tooth last week and my mom said if I request you, I can have a fresh, shiny and strong tooth as a replacement", said Miko with gleeful eyes. Toothy looked at him with amazement. It was a long time she saw such an innocent boy. With the advancement of science and technology fairy tales have lost their importance and kids nowadays don't even read fairy tales. Such a kid is rare.

"Yes! I can give you a fresh tooth but for that what will you give me in return?" asked Toothy jokingly. "Well! I do not have anything much just a few candies will that do? And also, my fallen tooth, my mom said you will ask for that".

"O, okayyy! I will take whatever you have for me" said Toothy with a smile. Miko carefully pulled out a handful of candies and the pouch which contained his tooth and handed them over to Toothy. All of a sudden it began to rain, and Toothy invited Miko to her nearby shelter inside the bark of the banyan tree. The house from inside looked nothing like a tree bark. It was much similar to what Miko's mom had told him about the house of the fairies. Toothy's house was very beautiful, decorated with hanging plants, pots of berries and colourful flowers. There was a bed, table and a chair made of wood and a kitchen which had a wooden stove and the utensils made of wood. Miko also spotted one rack in the corner. It was stacked with little jars, containing teeth of various shapes and sizes. Toothy carefully placed Miko's tooth in a jar and kept it there. "Do you keep all the teeth here?" asked Miko curiously. "Yes, do you want something to drink?"

"Herb juice, flower potion or berry smoothie?" asked Toothy as she plucked some berries from the small pot and entered the kitchen. "No no, I would like to go home. My mom will be tensed if I am out for long". "Well you can't go home till the rain stops, and yes I keep all the teeth stacked here and when it's needed I deliver them to the soil." Miko could not understand the meaning of delivering the teeth to the soil and looked at Toothy with a confused face. Understanding his confusion , Toothy said "The plants need minerals to grow and calcium is there in human bones and teeth… so the mother earth has entrusted her fairies and nymphs to maintain the ecology and plant more trees and keep the Nature healthy."

"So you mean to say there are more like you?" asked Miko. "Yes, of course. There are a bunch of us. The water nymph, the vegetation fairies, the air fairies, fire fairies and earth fairies and also the animal fairy and there are further subdivisions… my work is to handover the teeth to the vegetation fairy... I was entrusted with this work..." said Toothy while she stirred the herb potion in a wooden glass and placed the glass in front of Miko .Drink it, I know you're exhausted after a long day in school. Human schools are boring, anyways, finish up quickly, the truck that dropped you here will pass from the same place in an hour", said Toothy as she sat pulling a chair. "How did you know how I came here?" asked Miko. "Okay that's enough information for today, should leave something for the next time."

"Sure I will come again when my tooth falls again. But what about my new tooth, you did not give me that" asked Miko hurriedly and looking sacred. "O no, you don't have to be scared. Teeth takes time to grow and the berry and herb potion I gave you will help your tooth grow overnight and make it stronger, shinier and healthy than before" said Toothy with a smile on her face. After Miko finished his drink, waved goodbye and headed back to the main road and got a lift from a truck going to the city.

"Where were you Miko, its 6pm? Where did you go? I was frantically calling your friends" howled his moth er as she saw him entering through the door. "O my God, where have you been in this weather? And why is your uniform so dirty? Did you get soaked in rain?" came the question one after the other along with his mom's protruding eyes

"Mom. Mom… I was about to get into the bus and then saw a butterfly and chased it, it went near the forest and there I met the tooth fairy" said Miko, eliminating half of the truth. For a moment there was silence in the room. His mother gasped and said I will talk to you later. Go and have a bath. I will put the geyser on and keep your night clothes out." Miko went inside and freshened up and on the dinner table his mom told him "Look dear, fairy tales are just stories, they are not true. I tell them to you because you enjoy them … do not chase the imaginative creatures in the forest. Forest only has dangerous wild animals and poisonous insects."

"But mom I saw the tooth fairy, she is Toothy, she is so nice." defended Miko with a mouthful of pasta. "That's enough storytelling, Miko, just eat and go to bed, you have school tomorrow."

"Forget all these stuff and try using your imagination in your language class for better marks" scorned his mom with big round eyes and walked past the table with her empty plate. Miko stuffed the rest of his pasta in his mouth and licked the sauce off the plate and fork before leaving for bed. He understood although the adults love telling their kids stories about fairies and monsters they do not believe in them. Miko looked at his gum in the mirror and poked it to see if there was some growth of a new tooth. To his disappointment there was none and he went to bed. It was not until next morning when he found a baby tooth was visible inside the gum. He rejoiced and thanked toothy for the herb potion. He brushed his teeth and carefully cleaned the would-be born, yet little born tooth and then left happily for school.

4. Dear God

I don't know where you stay;

It must not be too far away.

Up above the sky so high-

I saw you when amidst the grass I lie.

Your castle among the smoky cloud,

Your presence there speaks out aloud.

I saw you looking down at me-
Making me feel blessed by thee.

"Tell me o God how you made me!"
I asked you with a curious glee.

You smiled and pointed to the sky,
To the space in the heavens high.

Filled with clouds of different shapes,
Which turned and twisted by your grace.

From a cloud I saw a ball-
Taking a shape like a baby and crawl.

Until in it grew a lovely face,
With eyes and ears and all the rest.

I recognized the face to be mine-
Reflecting the blessings and benevolence of Thine.

5. Best friends

Waking up in the middle of the night, I went towards Jeet's bed. He was as usual shivering at the end. Today was his second day of treatment for cancer. Mom and dad were telling me, this disease kills everyone, no one survives but I know Jeet will. I love Jeet a lot. He saved me from dying. I was born on a roadside garbage box, along with my other siblings. The first few days I could not see and when I opened my eyes for the first time, I saw the world. The strong rays of the sun, the feeling of cold air on my body, the bees flying around the garbage box and my mother who took care of us very well. We would often run across the road and play around.

It was one winter evening, a group of boys came and started playing with us. My mother was very friendly with everyone and never barked at anyone without reason. But the boys in the course of playing and feeding us, tied firecrackers in two of my siblings' tails and set fire on them. We were extremely scared to hear the crackers burst. My siblings were so shocked for a week, that tears rolled down from their eyes and they refused to sleep, eat or play. My mother started barking and following them and they ran away. That was the first time I understood how human beings were. From that day onwards we were always scared and were very careful as to not to come out openly during the daytime. My mother kept all of us behind the garbage box and went out to bring food for us.

This went on for a few weeks until one day, the group of the same boys attacked us. My mother was busy chasing two of them and the rest came and began putting my siblings inside a sack. I had to run for my life. When I saw a boy coming towards me. I was extremely scared. I did not know where to go but I kept running and running till I was out of their reach. When I looked around I saw that I was not only out of their reach but also out of my own known locality. I was in an unknown place which I did not know. I looked around and tried to return but I could not find my way back. I was extremely tired and hungry. I went to shop selling food and tried eating from the left-over plates that was discarded in the dustbin. I did not mean any harm to anyone but the shopkeeper chased me with a broom. I could not eat even a single bite. I kept on walking and walking till I was extremely fatigued. The weather started turning bad and there was a series of thunder and lightning. I was extremely terrified because I have never seen such phenomena. I ran to take shelter inside a garage and crawled under a car. I was feeling so cold, numb and hungry that sometimes I lost my senses. When I woke I found myself inside a basket with a soft blanket wrapped around me. I looked up and saw Jeet for the first time. I was extremely scared of human beings and so I jumped out of the basket and tried to run away but the door was locked and I did not know what to do. I tried standing there but I was shivering and frightened of the situation. Jeet was very gentle with me. He tried to calm me down from a safe distance. "Hello I am Jeet, don't worry, I don't mean to harm you. You are hungry I got some milk for you. You want to have it?" I stood there looking at the eyes of this little boy. He was the first human being to show me much love and affection. I felt much better than I was before Jeet pushed the bowl of milk in front of me and I slurped the milk hungrily. After I had finished half of it, I stood looking at him again. "I hope you feel better now. Calm down, do not fear anyone over here. We are all family. Stay here and be a good boy. Okay" saying that he left the room. I looked around myself. This is where a human lives. This is so beautiful and different from the open sky. I went near the bed, the table and sniffed at everything that was unique to me. They smelled very different too. I missed the smell of my home. I found many weird things lying around in the room. I did not know what they were but one of them started clapping when I accidentally stepped on

it. The room was filled with such interesting things to mess around with. There was one dog who sang and jumped when I tapped on his head. There was also a huge wall. Whenever I went in front of it, I could see a puppy like me on the other side. He always imitated me. Whenever I barked, he barked at me. It was much later that I came to know that's mirror which the humans use to groom themselves, and it was no other but myself, my own reflection.

As the time passed, I was extremely comfortable with the family. I missed my mother and siblings but the family were very kind to me and never treated me in a bad way. They would give me food of my choice. All of us would go on a holiday and pic nics during the winter months. We played so many games, favourite of which were throw and fetch with our most favourite red ball. I was having a very happy life until one day I came to know that Jeet was suffering from a disease that would kill him very soon. I never knew what it was and would only see mother crying to Jeet's father. They would often take Jeet out to the doctor and give him a lot of medicines after the meal. I could not understand what was happening but at that time I noticed Jeet was becoming weaker and weaker and often saw him falling terribly ill. Every time after returning from the doctor he used to be so ill that he needed his father's support to stand.

One day my mother hugged me and said 'Your little friend won't survive for long' and she started crying hysterically. I did not know what she meant by Jeet won't survive for long. I was looking at her in a blank manner and then I rushed towards Jeet's room.He was lying in bed resting his face on a pillow. He had turned absolutely pale. I kept the red ball beside and sniffed at him. He smelt like medicine. He looked at me and smiled and patted my head and dozed off to sleep. He could no longer play with me. It was even very difficult for him to stand but I did not know that one day he would leave me forever.

Next morning when I got up, I saw Jeet sleeping peacefully. He looked very calm. I climbed down the stairs and ate the breakfast my mother had kept for me and then went to the garden for a walk. A beautiful butterfly came and sat on my nose. It was a rare type. I had never seen such a kind before. It was yellow striped on a Prussian blue body. I began to chase it and went too far in the process. It was after going pretty far that I realised it will be late and I must return home. I turned back and began to run back home. I reached home it was almost late evening and I saw the door was locked. I did not know where everyone was. They would not leave me alone like this I thought. I decided to wait near the doorstep. It was almost at night when mother and father arrived. They had tears in their eyes and an ambulance followed them. I ran up to them "where have you been mum?" She looked at me, hugged me and started crying again. I did not understand what was happening and then I saw the hospital people pull out Jeet from the car. He was sleeping. I went towards him and barked loudly. "Hey what's wrong with you? Get up, are you okay?" This time no answer came and it was not until after some minutes I realised that Jeet was dead. The terrible disease took away his life and I was left all alone by myself. Since the day I had come in this house Jeet took care of me so well, that I often used to forget the fact that I miss my mother and my siblings and I had lost that friend today. Jeet was cremated in the symmetry down the lane.

I often visited him with mum and dad and sometimes I used to go there alone, sit near his Tomb and remember the happy days. "We will always be together Puff" that's what he used to say and now he left me. I was taken good care of by my mum and dad. They did not neglect me in any way. It was one summer evening when I went to the symmetry again, a month has passed since Jeet had left us. I walked up Jeet's grave. "Catch puff, bring it here, good boy" I could hear Jeet telling me to fetch the ball. "I miss you Jeet". Something came towards me and fell on my head and bounced towards the grave. It was the red ball.

6.The Sky

Sky!Sky!Sky!

Why so high?

Come down please

Let's fly.

Since the day born was I,

I looked at you being so high.

From my baby cradle where I played,

I would point at you and say hi!

As I grew a little old,

My birth story was told.

As my mom sat to feed me my meals;

She said I was born from your heels,

My hair was made from your clouds,

And my tears made from your rains.

I am a part of you as you are of me;

Although so far and yet so near,

We shall always be.

Sky! Sky! Sky!

Why so high?

Come down please

Let's fly.

7.Inspiration

Do not waste yourself,

Explore yourself to reach the highest peak.

From where when you look down,

You feel proud of who you were,

And what you are today.

Let the journey make you feel glad,

For not giving up, for not letting go;

And believing in yourself.

Because 'You' are your only believer,

You are your only mentor,

Friend, philosopher and guide.

Smear your body and soul,

With that inspiration.

That comes from your Master,

Who knows you better than you do!

Use every opportunity that knocks at you.

Reject every low feeling of incapacity, worthlessness and pro-
crastination.

As they divert your mind from your goal,

Of serving the Lord with your creation.

8. The Time Machine

Tito has been spending sleepless nights over the thought, of which place in history he should visit. He has spent the past week visiting the library in the history section trying to find, which is the most interesting phase in the past. And it was yesterday looking at a Gorilla toy in a shop window, he decided it would be more interesting to visit the age of the Apes or the age before human evolution. "It would be more interesting because I will be able to see the transformation as well" thought Tito.

Tito is a 12 year old boy, who has recently discovered his grandfather's time machine. His grandfather was a scientist who was working to create a time machine but he expired before it was introduced to the world or tested. The time machine was dismantled and kept after being packed in the store room of Tito's old house. It was during his visit and stay here he discovered it and after a month of reading and studying his grandfather's journal and notes he was able to fix the time machine again. And he was confused as to which place, he should visit. Although he wasn't sure whether the machine would work, he was ready with the place of his choice.

It was on the day when both his parents went out for work, he decided to put the plan into action. He asked his house help to give him his meal early and then retreated to his room telling them not to disturb him because he wasn't feeling well. He packed his bag with some snacks, the camera his dad gave him and a jacket. Tito peeped outside the door and sneaked into the store when he saw his house help was not to be seen around.

Tito looked at the machine with brightness in his eyes. It was a huge machine, resembling a mini submarine with a steel body and tempered glass as the front and two side windows. He had waited too long to use it. Today it was the day. "Grandpa would have been very proud of me", he thought. He pulled open the cover and connected the plug to the switchboard. The light of the machine blinked and the window in front displayed the spaces for the information of the location to be travelled. Tito put the necessary details, the name of the place, the year, latitude and longitude of the exact locations. It wasn't surprising that Tito had done a lot of research about the place where he wanted to visit. After putting in the necessary details, he pulled open the door and entered and locked the door behind. The machine began to vibrate as soon as he switched on the machine. But after a few minutes the vibration stopped. Tito was confused as to what was happening and after some time when he saw nothing is happening, he decided to climb out of it. But no sooner did he touch the door knob to open it the machine vibrated again and a sharp ray of light began to glow on the screen of the machine almost blinding Tito. He covered his eyes quickly with his hands, sweating profusely, not knowing what was happening. At that time, he wished he hadn't come here and done all these. But there wasn't any option of going back. He stood in the vibrating machine holding his breath till everything became quiet. Tito looked around and stepped out of the machine. It's unbelievable!

"Where am I? Which place is this?" Exclaimed Tito in amazement.

"The time machine really works!! I have reached some forest." Tito stopped there for some time and then plucked some large leaves to cover up the machine. Tito then started walking ahead trying to find any trace of habitation, "does anyone live here, or the apes?" wondered Tito, as he walked through the forest setting apart the thick twigs and leaves with a long stick. He was fascinated by the variety of insects and birds he saw. After a long walk for some time, he saw peels of banana skins all over the forest. "Yes! I found them. They must be near us." Tito began to walk excitedly and walked with great speed.

After some time, he reached a clear ground where he saw numerous apes hanging around. Some of them were adults who were basking in the sun with their babies playing around them. It seemed that Tito had reached an Ape land. Tito was happily watching them from behind the bush until he felt a loud thud behind him and saw a group of ape babies looking at him with wonder. Tito was nervous looking at them but thought of introducing himself "hello, I am Tito, I am from the 21st century. How are you all doing? Happy to meet you."

The babies were looking at him for some time and then one of them started screaming and immediately Tito was surrounded by large apes frowning at him.

"Hello, I am Tito. I am from the 21st century. See I mean no harm ...." Before he finished his sentence, the apes were carrying him to their shoulders.

"O God, listen to me please, excuse me." But none listened to him. The apes kept Tito gently on the ground. All the apes of the place had gathered to look at Tito. The apes were of different shapes and sizes. Some of them were eating bananas while looking at him, some maintained a safe distance from crowd and looked at him with fear. The babies were fearless. Some of them climbed at him, poked his belly and pulled his hair. Tito was very patient and gentle in dealing with them but the mothers didn't want to risk her babies and pulled them away. A group of notorious ones had taken his bag. They didn't understand at first how to open it. They shook it for some time and when they were convinced something was inside it, they tore the bag impatiently to acquire those things. They looked at everything with suspicion. One of them took the torch light and twisted and turned to see what it was and threw it with a jerk when it gotswitched on. Another one was looking at the compass and was very excited to find the stick inside when he moved. Another ape had acquired the chocolate and tore the packet to find some weird sticky brown thing inside. It smelled and licked it. Tito was having fun looking at them. "They are so cute and they are our ancestors" thought Tito.

Tito was looking around but he was always watched by some ape or the other. It was during dusk Tito was taken inside a cave. The cave was decorated with ferns, bushes and plants of different colours. After Tito walked deeper inside, he saw an army of apes waiting and there was a huge rock at a raised platform. "What are they going to do with me?" wondered Tito as he stood there blooking at all. After a moment another ape entered. The entire army of apes rose and bowed their heads. It seemed to Tito that he was older than the others and was wearing a crown made of banana peels and flowers. "This must be the leader or something." Wondered, Tito. After he took his seat, he looked at Tito for some time and then said "what's your name young boy?" Tito was shocked, an ape can speak like him.

"Amazed? Only I among all the others can speak like you."

"Yes, no, I mean, actually I never thought about it sir. It's a pleasure to meet you, your majesty. My name is Tito, I am from 21st century" replied Tito with deep reverence which he perhaps had never shown even to a human king.

"Ooh, 21st century, what is that exactly?" asked the king-ape with a confused look in his eyes. "My name is Jolo, you can call me that. You are our guest. Please feel free to stay here as long as you want, in return for some favours if you don't mind." "Certainly Jolo. I will be happy to help. But how can I, and also, I will have to return home today itself. My parents will be worried."

"You will get to know after some hours. Take rest till then and enjoy our hospitality." No sooner did Jolo uttered the words, than the apes again picked him up and carried him out. "I can walk as well. Why do they have to do this?" wondered Tito. He was taken to a shady place. The place was decorated with special wild flowers of beautiful fragrance. In one corner different fruits were stacked up. Tito thought it perhaps is a place for the entertainment of special guests. "But do the Apes have special guests? It happens in the human world; who knows perhaps this is the trend here as well" thought Tito. He was made to sit on a rock covered with bushes, ferns and soft leaves. Two apes came to him and started fanning him with the large coconut tree leaves. Two of them came with a large platter of fruits and offered them to him. Tito was having a gala time, he felt like the king of the jungle, like 'Tarzan' as he read in the comic or watched in the movie, or even better. Although the fruits were like normal fruits, Tito felt it tasted much better than the ones in the city. Tito saw three baby apes were looking towards him but was hesitant to come near him. But when Tito started acting friendly, they came near him and climbed on his lap and hung from his shoulders. Tito fed them bananas and they were very happy being friends with and playing with him. After a few moments a group of Ape was seen to walk towards him. They picked him up and began to walk towards the cave. Everything, except this action of theirs to carry him on their shoulders was irritating Tito. This time he was taken to some other cave which had various herbs and roots lying all over the place.

"Welcome to our herbal caves. This is where we treat the injured apes. I have called you here to discuss some matters of importance. Please have a seat."

"Yes, I can only see it. When your apes put me down. I can walk Jolo. I don't need to be carried around. Said Tito irritated.

"I apologize, Tito. It's their way of showing reverence to you. Why should our guest's feet fall on the ground?" Jolo made a gesture with his hands indicating to put Tito down.

"You see, I am the only one who can talk like you. I am undergoing a transformation if you see my tail. I do not have a tail. I used to have it when I was young but with time it shrunk inside my body. I did not know what was happening or what was wrong with me and with time I also could speak this different language. And with time I had gained some qualities which are absolutely different from that of an ape. When you were spotted for the first time it was due to my orders that you were bought in because I found similarity of what I speak with what you were speaking earlier. And yes! I would like to discuss something with you if you do not mind" asked Jolo looking at Tito with expectations in his eyes.

"Certainly of course you can ask me anything" replied Tito."You want to tell me something about how humans are. Do you think

I resemble your people?" enquired Jolo. "People in my time, that is the 21st century, look exactly like me." said Tito. "We are born babies then we grow into toddlers, then teenagers, then adults and then we become old and die. A complete life cycle for a human."

"Exactly similar to what happens here as well. But we don't look like you accept only me having a human speech like you. But tell me something, will I look like you after a few days?"

No Jolo it's not a matter of a day or two. It's a matter of years and centuries. And yes, you will start to look like me or us humans when you will and your kind undergoes a transformation. That is called evaluation of human beings. Human ancestors were monkeys and apes and with time they got transformed from apes to us humans. You and your kind will get transformed into being like me, like us, like humans.

"Why do we have to transform? What's wrong with being an Ape? We are happy like this" asked Jolo with sadness in his eyes.

It is a Miracle of nature. To make you a human, the superior of all species on Earth. Perhaps nature wants to give you a chance, to make you superior so you can make the Earth a better place to live in." saying this Tito thought how ungrateful the humans have become towards nature. They chop down trees, hunt down animals and pollute the environment.

After being quiet for some time Tito said "Jolo it is nothing to be scared of you know, it is very good to get transformed into a human. But do not ever adopt the bad qualities or negative traits of being a human." After some seconds of silence Tito again said, "I belong to the 21st century. I am your future standing in front of you. I have good qualities as well as bad. I have seen people who are benevolent as well as cruel and harmful. It is all about how you think and what you want to make yourself into. Animals are in stinctively kind and benevolent, and so are human beings. But the choice is always with you as to which side you want to choose."

"So, you mean there is nothing harmful about this transformation?" enquired Jolo. Not at all, nothing is harmful in it, Jolo and perhaps not this generation but your upcoming generations will start to transform and that has to be accepted.You have no choice." replied Tito patting Jolo'sback.

"How do you know so much about this?" asked Jolo. "I belong to the future. We have studied all these in our history books." "History! What is that?" "History is a subject that tells us about the past happenings. It is taught in schools of the 21st century. We study your transformation phase. It is called the history of the evolution of mankind. We all study about you and your species."

"Really we will all become famous?" asked Jolo

"And there will be many archaeologists who will be coming to your place and in other places where other apes lived to dig out your remains or skeletons many years after you have died to study and know about your species and how you transform and the nature of your physicality's. And that's how we get to know about you all in the future."

Jolo was so amazed that he was unable to speak. He kept staring at Tito. "Will the world move so fast as to get all the details about who lived a thousand years or more back?"

"Yes of course, definitely. We all know about Dinosaurs as well. Don't you know about them? They are ancient to you as well."

"No! we don't know about them but here and there sometimes we do find bones of huge birds. We considered them Monster Birds……." After a long discussion with Jolo it was time to go back home. He bade goodbye to all the Apes and also his baby friends promising, the king he would return again soon. The Time Machine took Tito to the 21st century leaving behind the age of raw human selves. Tito landed back in the store room from where he started his journey. He climbed out of the machine and covered it after plugging it out from the socket. He peeped out of the room and saw it was all dark around "that means my parents are not yet back" thought Tito let me quickly sneak into my room.

That night while unpacking his bag, he saw a bunch of bananas and some pears stuffed inside his bag. The thought of kindness and hospitality on the part of the apes filled his heart with joy. Tito had really a lovely time with the Apes and their young ones. He had felt that the peace and kindness that exists amidst the apes of the natural forest is more desirable and soothing for a soul than the conflicts and restlessness of the human apes of the concrete forest.

9. A Happy Home

Have you ever wondered?

How would it be to build a happy home?

Amidst the dark woods,

Where you will wake up hearing the chirping of the birds,

Or sometimes the shrill screeching of the wild parakeet,

As it flies across the lavender sky.

Have you ever wondered?

How would it be to build a happy home?

Amidst the green wood'swere

The wind blows, carrying the fragrance of the wild flowers,

And brushing through your soft hair and rosy cheeks.

Have you ever wondered?

How would it be to build a happy home?

Amidst the green woods in the solitude,

Uninterrupted by the hustle of the busy city,

Where the humming of the birds, pecking of the woodpecker,

Buzzing of the bees and the night insects

Replaces the noise of vehicles, machines and ringing telephones.

Where the sweet cool air from the spring side

Efficiently replaces the air mechanically cooled down by the
machines.

In this happy home you can sleep,

Looking at the night sky,

Beautifully adorned with Moon and Stars,

Giving much required rest as compared to the false ceiling
adored with fancy lightings.

In this happy home,

Life would be much simple and uninterrupted.

Even death here would be like returning to the womb of the
Mother.

From where you were once born and bloomed like a flower,

To be born again perhaps as a colorful butterfly.

10. Creating a Life

I do not hate anyone,

I am not rude to anyone,

Neither am I jealous of anyone,

Nor that I have ego.

All I desire is to create a beautiful life;

With only those people whom I would choose to be there,

With people who would make me feel worthy,

With people who would make me feel loved,

With people whom I would not have to fear of being back-
stabbed,

With people who would stand by me,

In my darkest times, in morning emptiness,

In midday restlessness and late-night insomnia.

The rest, they just exist;

And I always choose to set boundary or a wall of distance,

Between them and me.

And I feel that to be essential for my peace and happiness.

I do not hate anyone,

I am not rude to anyone,

Neither am I jealous of anyone,

Nor that I have ego.

I only wish to have a beautiful life;

Keeping it hidden and safe from toxic and negative people,

And filling it with only those,

With whom I can be myself.

11. RECONNECTING TO ONE'S ROOT

"No mom! I am busy, I will not go to Merupur this time during pujas" screamed Ronnie as he slammed the door behind him.

I am amazed at such behavior, Ronnie, that's what you all learn nowadays. You must …"the voice of Mrs. Chatterjee faded as Ronnie turned on a podcast. Ronnie, like any other teenagers, always felt his freedom was not appreciated by his parents. Like every year this year also his parents have arranged to go to Merupur, Ronnie's ancestral village for Durga puja. Ronnie always loved to go there when he was a kid but as he grew up, his circle enlarged and he felt old age traditions and customs are not up to the mark with reality. Although he visits there with his parents every year, he hardly attends any of the puja rituals. He found early morning rituals not as good and worthy as his sleep. So, he preferred sleeping and woke at noon when most of the puja was over. The rest of the day he would spend either by reading books or playing video games with his cousins who were no different from him.

This year it was different. None of his cousins were visiting due to their board exams but such an excuse was not applicable for Ronnie. So, he started to revolt against the injustice done to him. He decided that no matter what happens, he will not put his guard down this time.

Mr. Chatterjee, Ronnie's father was a man of strict principles and rationality. He disliked making anyone do anything against their choice. He believed that a person will do something only when he is convinced it is to be done. So, he told his wife "Let it be Sima, let him be alone and take some time for himself" and to Ronnie he said "son you will not be forced to attend family pujas if you are not willing to. We leave in a fortnight; you can stay back". But a mothers mind always cares about the safety of her child. She was unwilling to leave Ronnie alone. So, Mrs. Chatterjee tried hard to persuade her son but all was in vain.

Ronnie stood at the balcony and waved goodbye to his parents. He swelled with a feeling of pride. He felt happy for his achievement and contemplated that if ever there were an association for young adults he should be chosen as the President. Ronnie felt like an adult completely in charge and responsible for his own life. For the first few days he felt awesome. He played video games all day and even called for restaurant food both for lunch and dinner, which would never have been possible with his mom being around.

Everything was going as he wanted, till one day when he called up his friends to make plans for pujas. To his amazement it was only one day he could hang out with his friends and the rest of the days all of them were busy with their families. After keeping away the phone, he sat with his book but he kept on flipping over the pages and also his mind. He had no idea what he could do on the puja days, playing video games and Netflix was already starting to get boring now. He really wanted to do something different and special during pujas.

Suddenly the lights went off, "Didi please give me a candle." shouted Ronnie. The house help came with the candles and placed them on the tea table. After sitting for some time, he thought of going to his dad's study to rummage through the books. Ronnie walked up to the study and pushed open the door.

This place was an adventure land for Ronnie. His father was an avid reader and has many books of different genre. As a kid Ronnie used to come here often and pulled out books to read based on its cover. He smiled as he walked closer to the bookshelf. With the passing time not only were the books turning old but Ronnie's taste for them has also changed. He looked around and found some books which he used to love flipping through when he was a kid. He kept the candle on a coaster on the table and looked around the room. He used to love this place as a child. His mother often told him that when he was a toddler he often came crawling to this room and would pull down the books on the lower shelf. It was due to his fear the lower self-books were shifted up, to keep them out of his reach.

Suddenly his eyes fell on a box in the lower shelf. He pulled that out and recalled it was his dad's box which was pulled out of the loft, a year ago during flat renovation. He took the box and kept it on the table. He then pulled the chair to sit.

The box was made of cartridge paper. And on the lid, it was written 'Abhinash'. He opened the box and saw multiple things in it. It was like Pandora's Box.

He saw it many times around the house but never had the chance to grab it and explore what was inside it. Ronnie brought the candle closer and began pulling out the things. Amidst all the little things and small booklets of comics there was this journal of his dad for the year 1886. He kept aside the box and began looking at the journal.

20.02.1886

'No matter how old we grow, it is always important to keep closer to our roots. That gives us our identity and makes us unique. No matter how old we become there will always be a time when amidst everything we will feel lonely, in spite of having multiple friends around us we will feel lonely and crave for a home, a bed to rest, a cozy pillow to sleep and nothing in the world can replace that feeling.'

He turned to another page which read. 'It is human tendency to fall in love with something which belongs to others but equally difficult is to even like what's our own.'

Suddenly the call from their house breaks the attention of Ronnie. The electricity is finally back. He puts off the candle and takes a closer look at the things inside the box. He finds a small scrapbook-like thing and flips through its pages. His dad had created this scrapbook when he was in college. Ronnie's dad often told him how terrible homesick he used to feel during his college days. The scrapbook contained black and white pictures of his dad's childhood days at Merupur. How he celebrated each and every festival and a little note written beside it. It captured the essence and happiness of every festival which his dad had celebrated as a kid. There were pictures of Rath yatra, JhulanUtsav, Janmashtami, Annakut, Durga puja, Village fairs and others.

Suddenly Ronnie's eyes fell on a picture where his dad was holding a blue necked bird in his hand. Ronnie remembered his grandma used to call him up on Dashami day to see the flying ritual of 'the Nilkanth bird." "What's there in watching a bird flying,

Thammi?" Ronnie used to say with sleepy eyes and again doze off to sleep. The more he saw the pictures the more he was longing to go to the puja. With the last picture of his grandma and her other village women giving 'Alpona' in Kojagori Laxmi puja, Ronnie kept the scrapbook and the journal inside the box and then kept the box in its place. He rushed to his room and called up his dad

"Hello dad. I was saying that will it be a problem to send the car tomorrow. I was thinking of going there and attend the pujas."

His dad smiled and spoke with a satisfaction "sure beta, the car will be there for you. Travel safely. We will be waiting."

12. Incomprehensible You

What you are to me is impossible to show,

You are the treatment of my mind when it feels low.

You are the beautiful dream,

Unlike the nightmare which makes me scream.

You are like the secured place in the mother's womb,

A new life passing in from an old tomb.

You are like the first consciousness with the first breath in the
operation table,

Unlike the vaccination pains to make the future health stable.

You're like the first pillow to sleep peacefully on,

To hold my soft head when alone.

You're like the side pillow to climb and sleep,

You are the wonderful surprise that makes me leap.

You are like the first new toy which was my first best friend,

Most dear with whom life can be spent.

You are my first chocolate sweet and tasty,

You are like the first bite of the chocolate pastry.

You are like the first nursery teacher,

Who taught me with care all alphabets, numbers and their features.

You are like my innocent trust,

Which believed Santa's gift is a must.

You are my first love that is always ever youthful and fresh,

You are like that happiness and amazement in life's every phase.

You are like every first experience in the days of growth,

You are my first love or the magical dream or both.

13. Self-Made

Lata stood in front of the glass wall and was reminiscing about the past. She had recently purchased this flat in the memory of her parents who are no longer there with her. Her dad always wanted her to settle down well and then built her own house. She looks up at the sky and feels her dad would feel proud of her if he would have seen her today. Lata has come a long way. It wasn't easy to fight the society especially as a girl, her father was an artisan in the small village of Jabalpur and as it happens in the interiors, where the girls are married off at an early age. She was also excellent in artisan work and even sculpting. Mud was her favourite toy when she was a toddler. She felt like God when she could create something out of it. She went to school and both her father and her grandfather supported her desire to get educated, but later it was stopped as she turned 16. Marriage proposals began to come and a boy was selected for her. None asked her how she felt or even if she wanted to get married now. Her consent was not required.

She once asked her father "do you really want me to get married?"

Her father was quiet for some time then said "I really want you to choose a life for yourself, getting married or not I wish it was your choice but we do not have the means to be so assertive." Lata did not argue over the point. She was not willing to get married now but she had no choice. It is often said that we do not decide what we want for ourselves but someone else does. And it was on the day of the marriage her parents failed to arrange for the dowry demanded by the groom's family and as a result the boy was taken away from the marriage ceremony. It was a very hard time for the family and nobody stood beside them. Lata's family was very poor and turned absolutely bankrupt in the process of arranging money for Lata's wedding. Lata's mother cursed her, day and night and wished that she must drown herself in the Ganges. It was only a few months prior to Durga Puja that orders for the Durga Idol and additional decorations required during the Puja began to come in. Lata's family was mentally broken but they had no choice; they had to work in order to meet hunger. Lata was also willing to help but her mother was angry and said "please let it be, you did enough for us". Lata did not understand what her fault was if the groom backed out at the last moment. She was extremely hurt by her mother's behavior. She retired quietly to the one corner of the workplace and sat looking at what her father was doing. After a while it was out of sheer boredom she started tossing around a blob of mud and tried to create shapes of utensils. She was not an expert artisan like her father but she was gifted. She created beautiful plates, dishes and bowls from the mud and even small dolls and showpieces. But all she kept hidden. Because her mother once scolded her "why are you wasting the raw materials like this? What are we supposed to do with those?" Since then, Lata never displayed her art. Not even her father knew.

It was only during the selling time the buyer of the zamindar's house noticed the clay utensils and the dolls. He asked, "Who made those? Are they for sale?" "My daughter made them. But it's just her hobby. We never thought of selling them. You can buy it if you want, "Said Lata's' father. Apart from the idol, the dolls were also sold to the zamindars of the village, whose daughter enjoyed collecting dolls of different types. Days passed, Lata kept on learning sculpting techniques from her father and reading books from her neighbors who went to school. She was a quick learner, that's why she could remember a lot of things after one or two reads.

One day a man knocked at the door of Lata's house. "Ma'am, Mr. Roy said that he will be arriving here in 10 minutes", said

Lata's secretary. "Okay, please place orders for the last batch of goods," said Lata. She walked away from the window and sat on her sofa. The man was unknown. "Is this the house of Lata?"

"Yes, it is I am her father." "Hello, I am a friend of your Zamindar babu. I saw your idol. It was very nice. Then I saw the dolls made by your daughter. Can I see some more of her work?" "Sure, Lata, bring and show some of your work to babu", asked her father.

When Lata bought and handed over the items to babu. He was looking at them very carefully. He turned and looked at the dolls from every angle and ran his fingers tracing the immaculate details. He was very impressed with the work and said, "I am an artisan myself. I have business in Mumbai and I was very amazed to see the dolls made by Lata in zamindar's house. I have an offer for Lata. I would like Lata to join my workforce. And don't worry, my workforce has many women and girls of Lata's age and older. If she joins me, I will pay her 10000 a month plus food and stay for free." said the man.

Lata's father was amazed he did not know how to react. He was overwhelmed but was a little scared as to how to let go of his daughter so far off. He looked at Lata who was also shocked and confused. "You don't have to decide now. You all discuss and let me know. I will be here for a week." the man left after appreciating Lata some more. That night Lata's' dad asked her "do you wish to go my dear?"

"I wish nothing, baba. I love making new things and if I am given the chance to learn more and then contribute to the family income, I would like to go." replied Lata.

Next day, Lata and her father went to the zamindar's house and met Mr. Dutta and informed him about Lata's willingness to join the work. It was only two days later Lata and her father would leave for the city with Mr. Dutta. The news of Lata's new job spread like a wildfire and the village people began to resent stating the city jobs are bad, especially for a young girl like Lata. It was during this time when Lata spoke on behalf of herself. She said "when I was supposed to get married and the groom's party left due to the shortage of money, none of you stood by my family. I was called unlucky so today when this unlucky girl is leaving the village it's good for all right? Why does anyone care?" The people were stunned at her prompt reply. Lata was so quiet suddenly it was unacceptable for others that she should speak out like this. After a lot of argument, the neighbors were forced to retreat to their homes and the next day Lata started her journey for the new life. She was mesmerized looking at the big city, the crowd of people and vehicles of different types amazed the little girl who belongs to the village. She reached the workshop area and saw so many people working there. She was very interested to see how the people work there. After a few rounds, she was taken to the quarters where the employees stayed. She said goodbye to her father with tears in her eyes and promised to work hard as per her capacity. Lata was a quick learner; she learnt what the trainers taught her and with time she became the most artistic and creative artisan of the batch with her employer Mr. Dutta. He was very fond of her and praised her to boost her confidence. One day Mr. Dutta bought the news of an international competition. He wanted three of his best artisans to participate in the competition. Lata was one of them. She was very nervous in the beginning but then she tried her best to create the best of what she could and it was her things that won the first prize of $25000. Lata was extremely happy and tears came in her eyes. Finally, she could prove to herself that she was not worthless, she was not a loser or unlucky as a girl. The money that Lata had won was a huge sum and it was under the guidance of Mr. Dutta she formed a small workshop and a shop of her own for making her own little things for sale. As the time passed, she started selling extremely well and her handmade items included dolls, utensils, idols of various shapes and sizes and other decorative pieces of the household. At first, she had only one shop to work with but as she began to make profit, she hired shops at the export fair. Tie-up her project with branded selling companies and started selling to the international buyers as well. In this endeavor, she attracted a lot of foreign clients who appreciated Lata's designs on the potteries and other artworks that displayed rich Indian culture and heritage. She was an expert at analyzing the buyer's taste. She understood no matter how indifferent the Indians were to their own culture, crafts and art works, foreigners are more interested in knowing about them. She not only created the designs to be painted on the potteries and other goods, she would also work to create the designs on the actual base.

As she started making more profit, she turned her interest towards social welfare as well. She made the woman artisans a part of her work force. She herself trained them and helped them get empowered by earning their own money. Within four years her business started spreading rapidly. She used to send a lot of money home and also made it a point that her parents repaired the old house where they lived. She also forced her father to give up working and take time to relax. This good fortune of Lata's family made the neighbors very jealous and they started pointing at the fact that perhaps Lata was involved in some immoral activity which fetched her a lot of money instantly. Lata was absolutely indifferent to what was said against her but her family especially her father could not accept such remarks against her daughter. It was out of frustration and stress he passed away in a cardiac arrest. On knowing about her father's departure, Lata rushed to her village to see her father for the one last time, but the ruthless villagers were not allowing her to be a part of the rituals. It was the Zamindar who spoke in favor of Lata. "If you do not allow her to stay here, I will call the police and get you all arrested." Lata broke into tears. She could not believe that in such a ruthless world, nicer souls also exist. She attended the last ritual of her father. Looking at the funeral fire burning in front of her, Lata was completely broken. Her father was her only source of encouragement and moral support for any new work. She stayed in the village for a week and then brought her mother and grandfather with her to the city. Her grandfather could not bear the shock and passed away within a week of coming to the city and her mother passed away exactly after a year of her father's departure. Lata was now completely alone with only Mr. Dutta, as her official guardian in the city, whom she respected as a father and guide. Lata was now a successful woman and an entrepreneur running over five showrooms in two cities and her works sold in international stores including craft hubs in the airport, but she was alone and lacked the warmth of her near and dear ones. The only thing that got her going was the feeling that no matter wherever her parents were, they were extremely proud of Lata and how she had made herself and she is also contributing for others through her business.

A knock was heard on the door. "May I come in Ms. Lata?"

"Yes. Please" "Good evening. I am Mr. Animesh from Star Magazine. I took an appointment for today's interview." "Oh, yes Mr. Roy! Please, have a seat." "This interview is for the Star Magazine 2011, special issue for young entrepreneurs. I have some questions for you Ma'am." Lata nodded apprehensively. "To what do you owe your success?" "To misfortunes and pain." "I am sorry, I didn't understand" "Misfortunes and pains are the triggers to stubbornness to do something better for yourself. When a person is happy, they tend to be very average with their lives because their life is okay and they become absolutely contented with that."

The reporter smiled and went on with the next question "So to what human factor do you owe your success?"

"My father and Mr. Dutta. They have always helped me and encouraged me to be what I am today. And of course, my employees without whom reaching the target sale would never have been possible." "So, you mean to say if Mr. Dutta wasn't there you would not have been what you are today?"

"I am grateful to Mr. Dutta for everything and all the opportunities he gave me and the faith he had in me. He was one who saw talent in me." "What are your hobbies Ms. Lata?" "I love painting in my free time and I like to revisit my past and the past success to encourage me in future." "What makes your art work different from the others in the market?"

"My love for the country, culture and its heritage.Today everyone is busy imitating the west, everything one does is either directly taken from them or has the influence of the west. I believe my love for the roots and the influence I derived from it gets appreciated by my buyers."

"And how is your business different from the ones already there?"
"Initially when I had started, I used to work only for profit, but with time I realised there were many like me in the society who suffered because they had no income. So, it was then I promised myself that I would do anything in my capacity to lift them up as well. My business is not only a profit making organization, it's also a dream, an effort for the wellbeing of others like me."

As the interview continued the blazing hot golden chariot of the Sun God is seen to be moving slowly towards the other side of the Earth, after witnessing the success of a woman who has successfully created light out of darkness not only for herself but also for others.

14. Looking Within

Close your eyes and look,

What do you see?

The world, the sky, the birds, the people?

Nothing but only you;

The dark layers

Of your undiscovered soul.

The dark realms of yourself,

Lost amidst the noises of everyday chores, talks,

Arguments and other distractions.

Sit calmly, take few deep breaths,

Try to pay attention to every minute movements and ripples of your mind.

Try to not give in and fight back.

All the temptations that hold you back,

And prevent you from probing deep down at yourself.

For the fear the silence and calmness

Which might dig up the uncomfortable memories

Which we desperately try to avoid,

Seeking refuge in distractions of all kinds.

It was, is and will always be a pull between calmness and desire
to move.

Enslaving the mad elephant had always been a war,

Once successfully done then 'You' can find the way

To a giant ball of white light within,

Which is the real YOU, the 'Satchidananda', the pure bliss,
consciousness.

Forever happy, forever satisfied.

Surrounding yourself with that light-

You will gain the immense power to break through the cage,

Escape and merge into the cosmos of eternal peace.

15. Childhood

You have never lived your childhood

If you have not been confused as a baby,

Looking at your own reflection in the mirror.

You have never lived your childhood

If you have not secretly dropped,

The boiled vegetables given by your mom,

Out of the window for the birds to eat them for you.

You have never lived your childhood

If you have not sung the title song,

Of Your favourite cartoon show,

When it was played on the TV,

And jumped with happiness,

At the sight of your favourite cartoon.

You have never lived your childhood

If you have not blown air into the soda,

Through a straw.

Or tried to catch the rainbow soap bubble,

When it was blown out of the bubble ring.

You have never lived your childhood

If you have not chased a butterfly or a dragonfly,

As they danced from one flower to another.

Or hop into the rain puddles

While returning from school.

You have not lived your childhood

If you haven't thrown paper rolls,

On your classmates and friends.

Or you haven't cried hanging on your mother's sleeves,

To get you the fancy toy or stationery,

Displayed outside a shop's window.

You have not enjoyed your childhood

If you have not desperately peeped out of the window,

After the rain, searching for the rainbow.

Or, figuring out faces amidst,

The ever-changing shapes of the clouds.

You have not lived your childhood

If you haven't counted the new clothes,

Multiple times during the festivals.

Or, found packed gifts beside your bed on Christmas Eve,

And believed in the existence of Santa clause.

You have left behind everything, except memories;

Which proves that you have lived a certain stage of life to its
fullest.

Re thinking of which brings smile on your face,

When you feel like giving up.

At times of disappointments and agony,

Which life throws at you to test your

Patience, endeavor and love for living.

16. The lovers

Siddhartha laid the coffee cups in the tray and poured the black coffee in them. He heard the sound of the toast popping up from the toaster behind him. He kept the freshly toasted bread on the plate and pulled out the jar of hide and seek and carefully, laid them in the plate. He turned off the gas where he was cooking two sunny side up. Siddhartha then arranged all the breakfast components in a serving tray and walked towards Rima's bedroom. He knocked at the door and as usual, finding no response he walked straight inside the room. He kept the serving tray in the table nearby and pulled apart the curtains allowing the fresh sun rays to enter and touch Rima's face. She was in deep sleep. Siddhartha stood looking at her fresh Lily-like face. He kept on looking at her remembering the first time he had met Rima.

It was on the first day of office that both of them had picked up a fight. Rima was a graphic designer and Siddhartha joined the team of the content writers. They both were paired up by their bosses to work together which was the most difficult task for them. However, they did survive working together without killing each other. It was only a matter of a time when they had realised that there is more than friendship to their relationship. It was only during the hard times one can spot true friends. It was during Rima's family crisis after the death of her father, Siddhartha was the only one standing by her. He had helped her acquire the death certificate, helped her with the bank work and shifted from the flat Rima and her mother was leaving to a flat of a much lesser rent. As the time passed Rima was becoming more dependent on Siddhartha and trusted him more than anyone else. It was on Rima's birthday that Siddhartha proposed to her at her favourite restaurant. It was only a month before their wedding Rima met with an accident while returning from the office. All the hopes and happiness of both the families were shattered, when it was discovered that Rima had lost her memory. She did not remember who she was and what she was doing in the nursing home. Her mother cried day and night and it was only after a few months Siddhartha's family began to resent him being still in touch with Rima but he didn't leave her alone. He took a job in another city and then shifted there with Rima, who was unable to recognize who Siddhartha was but with time she realised that whosoever he was, he wasn't harmful and that even though she could not remember who she was, he genuinely loved her, his eyes said it all.

Today was their anniversary and it's being almost a year since Siddhartha was trying hard to help Rima to recover her memory. Rima woke up stretching herself like a baby. "How come you woke up so early? We slept late yesterday."

"Just like that. Come, wake up, I have made you breakfast. Your favourite breakfast. And also, your favourite flower bouquet. Rima turned her head and looked towards the side table.

"It is 5th October today, our anniversary right." "Yes, it is you remember?" "No, I remember only the date but I do not remember the significance of the day." said Rima as she looked down. They both remain quiet for some time and then Siddhartha breaks the Silence.

"It's ok, you will remember in time. I won't give up on you." "Don't you think you are wasting your time with me, who does not even remember who you are or what relationship we share?" "If I were in your place Rima, would you do the same? Leave me alone and go?" "I do not know that because I cannot feel anything towards you but……." "Let it be. Okay! Don't force your brain. It will start to hurt again. Let's finish breakfast and get ready. We are going out for lunch." "Okay sure but you have your office today, right?" "I took a leave. I also deserve a leave, right?"

Rima smiled and asked "So where are we going?" "Let's see. Some new cafe has opened up nearby let's go there and then we will visit the fair near it." "The fair?" asked Rima with her eyes popping.

"Yes, there is a fair taking place in High Square. Enjoy the day like it is. Okay." Rima loved the plan. She really wanted to enjoy going out for a change. After breakfast, both of them were dressed into their best outfits and walked out of the door. At first, they went to the restaurant and ordered some delicious warm Chinese food. While munching on the gravy noodles Siddhartha asked "so how is the food? Do you like it?"

"I think it's really nice. We should sometimes pick up food from here and have dinner or lunch." replied Rima, while picking up a chicken piece from the sizzling hot serving tray.

"I like your idea picking up food as well." said Siddhartha.

After a minute or two of silence, Rima asked "why are you doing this for me, Siddhartha? You know I don't know what relationship we are in and I do not remember anything about the past but the things that you do, makes me feel very special and also makes me feel that I am doing injustice to you" said Rima with sadness in her eyes.

Siddhartha looked into Rima's eyes and said "it does not matter if I am doing this for you for now. If I have to I would do it for as many years as it is required. I do not regret it. The time which I am spending with you is the best time of my life", the arguments ended there. It was not the first time that Rima had brought this up and tried to convince him that she will perhaps never get well or remember him. So, it is better he chooses someone else for himself or have a life of his own but Siddhartha refuses to give up. It takes one to be very brave to cling on to something without any response but only with a positive hope. Siddhartha was one of those brave souls, too stubborn to give up. After they had finished eating, they walked out of the restaurant and took a cab to the fair. The fair was beautifully decorated. It was so colourful that both Siddhartha and Rima remember their childhood days. There were merry-go-round, roller coasters, carousel, bumper cars, the mechanical bull and many other types of rides whose names were unknown to them. Apart from the rides, there were other games like shooting which enabled you to win prizes. First Siddhartha and Rima went for the giant roller coaster ride. Although Siddhartha and Rima were extremely excited to go for the ride initially, as the ride started to move up and then descend down, they began to feel giddy. But both Rima and Siddhartha sat side by side holding each other's arms. It was only in one moment when the ride was high that Rima saw flashes of her past in front of her eyes. It was so sudden that she did not know what was happening or even did not get the time to tell Siddhartha. But such flashes came to her multiple times as the ride moved up.

After the ride ended, she told Siddhartha what has happened to her.

"It is okay, never mind you always see flashes of memory coming in an unexpected time. That's what your doctor told. Don't worry about it. If it is meant to be remembered, you will remember it. Do not put too much pressure" said Siddhartha looking hopeful. They decided to try the balloon shooting game. They both tried their hand in it and Siddhartha laughed at every failed attempt by Rima. However, since they could burst all the required number of balloons the shopkeeper gave Rima a small key ring and that small gift made her extremely happy. After an hour of roaming and enjoying the fair treats, Siddhartha was tired and wanted to return home but it was on Rima's request he agreed for another ride.

"Something light, this time please. Not rowdy as the roller coaster. I can't take that sort of shaking anymore. I will puke" exclaimed Siddhartha. Rima chuckled and said "okay let's go for a swing ride."

That swing from one site to another and rotated when in the middle. That was a little less crowded as compared to the other rides in the fair. Only ten people who could be accommodated at one time and Siddhartha and Rima were two of them. When the ride began initially it was alright. But all of a sudden in the middle of nowhere the screw of one of the leavers got loosened and the entire Ride came crashing on the ground. Although it was not such a high ride, people were injured. Both Rima and Siddhartha, because they were sitting on the sides, got injured in their heads and were taken to the nearby hospital. It was only after five hours that Rima gained her consciousness and felt extreme pain in her head. Within a minute of opening her eyes, she could remember everything of her past life, how she had fallen in love with Siddhartha, how Siddhartha had helped her and her family and how she had an accident and lost her memory. She rushed to the doctor asking for Siddhartha the doctor told "he is admitted in the ICU because of his head injuries were ma jor." Tears rolled down her cheeks and she felt absolutely lost.

"Even when I remember everything, I do not have the person in proper health to share my happiness with" she started crying standing in front of the ICU. The doctor patted her back and led her back to her room. Everything will be fine, Miss Rima, please rest for a bit. You also have injuries. Any updates about Mr. Siddhartha will be conveyed to you."

Rima silently wept lying in her bed. Her head was paining like hell but she didn't pay attention to it. She silently prayed to God for Siddhartha's wellbeing. It was after 72 hours the doctors informed her that Siddhartha is back in senses and she can talk to him tomorrow. At night Rima could not sleep well. She was extremely anxious to meet Siddhartha, hug him and tell him that she is fine.

"All the hard work that you had put after me did not go to waste" thought Rima, as she was extremely grateful to God for making him fall in love with Siddhartha. The next morning Rima rushed to Siddhartha. She stood looking at him for some time and ran her fingers through his hair. She felt as if she found her true self after a long time. Siddhartha opened his eyes which were blurry, tired and exhausted. Rima told Siddhartha with tears in her eyes "looks Siddhartha, I am standing in front of you. I remember everything. I remember everything. My memories came back. You will be fine soon and then we will go home together. Okay. I love you. How are you feeling now? Is it still that painful? "Yes, a little bit, but I am sorry, do I know you, who are you?" exclaimed Siddhartha all confused.

17. You are alone But It's A Good Thing

You are alone, absolutely alone

Amidst the room full of people,

Parents, relatives, friends and neighbors.

You are alone, at the middle of the night

Staring at your social media in your phone,

Thinking about how good it would have been to talk to someone.

But over 300 friends there are just acquaintances not confidants!

You are alone, in your bed

Tossing and turning in the early mornings,

And suffering from that vast emptiness.

Deep within your heart,

All you need is a warm hug,

By someone who can tell

"I need not know why you feel this,

But the pain will pass and till then I am there".

But that's a dream

You are all alone, in your success

Amidst a room full of people,

Whose fake smile does not cover their green eye.

You are alone, in your failure

Surrounded by people laughing in their minds,

But sympathizing in front telling every means to show,

They care about you more than you would for yourself!

You are alone, and you are your own best friend and that's a good thing.

Find the happiness within you.

Just like a mask deer content with the sweet smell,

Of its own body and remains forever content,

Without depending on any external cause.

Or like flowers with all its nectar,

Find satisfaction in your heart.

Fall in love with yourself,

With every aspect of yourself that you hated earlier

Acceptance and love, the two keys to self-satisfaction and peace.

18. MIRA – The Spiritual Lover

The sunrays fell on her face and touched her matted locks of uncombed hair. Mira woke up looking at the face of her beloved. To her the face of Krishna bore more rays of hope than the sun. She smiled shyly at him and sat on her knees. The nights were spent in ecstasy as she sang to make her lord sleep. It was her usual routine to sing as he ate and then to put him to sleep. Last night was nothing exceptional. She cooked rice pudding and decorated it with some wild berries on top. She has an immense pleasure while presenting the supper to him which felt as if her Kanha liked the food. She sang till her heart contained and wiped the hands and face of Kanha after he finished his food to make him sleep. She would continue to sing as the tears rolled down her cheeks and fell on the blue lotus feet of Kanha and then she slept on his feet. It was amazing how she felt at peace as she slept on his feet. It seemed as if she was sleeping like a baby on a satin pillow.

This morning she felt an extreme urge to make a pink flower garland for her Kanha. She went to the garden and began searching for the pink flowers. After walking for some time she did find a plant bearing beautiful pink flowers. The moment she looked at them she realised that it was meant for her lord. She walked towards them with gleeful eyes of a child. She looked carefully at each flower. It was her way of choosing the perfect and flawless flower for her beloved. She found some which would be worthy of being worn by her Kanha but the moment she tried to pluck one she saw the beautiful blue pearl like face of Krishna on the flower. She was stunned looking at them. All of them bore the face of her beloved. She touched the flowers with her soft hands, tears rolling down her eyes. It was not the first time that she saw and felt the pres ence of her beloved amidst nature. But today it was something different. She realised it was very childish of her to present her lord the things which belonged to him, of which he was himself a part and whole. In spite of looking at this eternal truth which takes an ordinary human million births to realise, Mira still wanted to present her beloved with the wild pink flower garland but how can she pluck the flowers, it would hurt them and his Kanha too. Finding no other way, she sat on her knees and prayed to them.

"Dear Lord, I am your servant for life and eternity. I am too insignificant to understand your existence and I never try to do either for that would be foolishness on my part. I am happy that I get to see you and serve you day and night and sing in your praise. The realization that you wanted to bestow on me today makes me grateful, but I do not want such realizations Lord which prevents me from serving you, which prevents my petty human eyes from seeing you beautifully ornamented with my chosen flowers, and which prevents me from that beauti ful feeling of your presence when you lick up the last bits of rice pudding that I try to make for you. I am happy to be just your insignificant servant Lord. Do not deny me that privilege by bestowing on me such deeper realizations" begged Mira. Warm tears of love and gratitude rolled down her tanned cheeks.

It seemed that the lord heard her prayers. The flowers fell, on its own, on the lap of Mira. She looked in amazement and joyfully thanked her Kanha. She knew he would never deny her request. She carefully collected all the flowers as if touching her Kanha himself and kept them in her earthen dish. She happily ran towards the temple and sat to make a garland for her lord.

She sang a song of praise while making the garland. Soon the temple was surrounded by birds, monkeys and other animals who heard her with rapt attention. They were mesmerized and did not move or create any noise so as to disturb her. After some time, some birds flew in with a Tulsi branch on their beak filled with fresh green Tulsi leaves. Mira saw the leaves and looked at the birds with her calm eyes. The animals were not afraid of her. It was as if a whirlwind of realization which circled around the lord's temple, which touched every life. The realization of all being one, all being a part of Him touched every mind present there, so there was no need for anyone to fear anyone. They were all friends and servants of the same lord who created them out of himself. After making the garland. Mira wetted the end of her saree and wiped the face, arms, legs, feet and hands of the lord and put the garland around his neck.

Everyone including Mira looks at their Master with utter astonishment and pleasure of an innocent little child at the sight of his mother. Standing there in the wooden unpolished altar of broken twigs and branches, was the blue hued Lord of the universe. Adorned in the yellow-colored garment and pink flower garland, bracelets and armlets made him look like the Sun at dawn which is mild yet powerful, which soothes the soul looking at it and denotes the beginning of life.

Mira kept staring at him and his smile with a sense of satisfaction and joy in her heart till she realised it was the time for her to sing again.

"O graceful Lord of the universe shower your grace on us like the fresh rain on the dry soil…" sang Mira closing her eyes. Her soul seeing the smiling face of her beloved Lord reflected in her heart.

19. Everything Makes Sense at the End of the Day

I have often wondered why the life

Throws miseries at me?

Making me feel lost and confused,

Resisting my movements, no further than a couch.

And thoughts to the boundaries of negativity.

I have often wondered why,

Out of the millions of people inhabiting the Earth;

I am the most sensitive one.

Always travelling on an Emotional Roller coaster.

I have always wondered why,

Am I the one to losefavourite people?

To soon, remaining only as memories

And cheated by the remaining,

On whom I have started to depend.

I have always wondered why can't I have A peaceful weekend interrupted by

Anxieties and depression and fears

Resulting from overthinking.

After I was broken multiple times,

I realized that I was fixed.

Fixed up to a level where breaking did not hurt

Or perhaps nothing was left to be broken.

One day, I felt so bowed down and tired-

That I was no more bothered by what was going on around me.

Now I realise, I was trained mercilessly by Life.

With every emotion of fear, anxiety and hopelessness,

Felt by me to its extremity.

Then I turned absolutely indifferent to every emotion

Caused by minor things of life.

With every agony I was made to suffer,

I turned rock solid, impenetrable by grief and pain

With every person stabbing me at back and losing the ones I loved.

I was able to detach myself from every reason that disturbs my sanity;

And here I stand at the end of the day,

Strong, unbreakable and invincible.

Thanking life, and its sufferings

For teaching me the art of indifference and being happy.

20. 'Death', a Reason to Live

Daksha stared at the email message on her computer, her mind racing so fast that the words blurred together and no longer made any sense. Just three lines, but enough to make her life. The life she had worked so hard and sacrificed so much to build. It began to crumble around her, she felt helpless as to what she would do next. It was not something which she didn't expect. The email was from her doctor friend, which declared her grandfather was suffering from brain tumor. It was sudden, he was fine when she left for the USA last week. He came to the airport, bid her farewell and wished her a happy journey. She was efficient in work and her company selected her for conducting a deal with the foreign clients. It was an important stage in her career which she was thankful to have and her further promotion depended on it. The email she received made her dumb to the time and existence. She could not understand where she was standing and her future mission for which she was there. Her mind produced millions of thoughts at the same time, especially thoughts about the most important person in her life, her grandfather.

Daksha's parents died when she was two, her grandfather played the role of both the parents and never made her feel the need of her parents. He was the one to manage the house, take care of Daksha, work hard to meet her little needs and give her a better education. "I would make you proud one day Dadaji" little Daksha used to say. And her grandpa would happily take Daksha in his arms and toss her in the air. All the past memories were projected in her mind screen, it squeezed her heart, oozing the last drop of tears from her eyes. She felt like the only person on earth, broken and helpless. She forgot all about her client meeting the next day. Job and career for which she has worked so hard seems insignificant now. Her only desire was to go back to her grandfather, hug him and say "don't worry Dadaji, I will be there with you and you will be fine soon". She came to the USA on Monday. On Thursday her grandfather suddenly fainted in the park where he visited every morning to meet his friends. When he regained consciousness, his friends dropped him home and called Daksha. "Dadaji what happened? Are you feeling ill? Did you forget to take your blood pressure medicine?" ''No dear I am fine, no need to panic" assured her grandfather. Daksha had no peace perhaps because she was away and could not see her grandfather's condition. She called up one of her friends, Rima who was a doctor and asked her to take charge for a complete checkup of her grandfather. "Hey Daksha, yesterday I went to your grandpa for a complete checkup. He seems to be fine. But I suggest a brain scan as soon as possible" stated Rima over telephone. Since, Daksha was away she requested her friend to do the needful as early as possible. But it was the brain scan report that almost destroyed her life.

She was so grief stricken, that she failed to realise her phone was ringing. It was Rima, ``hey Daksha! listen I know it's not the time to console you or give you any false hope but it's a brain tumor." The other side was so silent that Rima could hardly hear Daksha breathing.

"Hello Daksha! hello!Are you there?" asked Rima. ``Yes, tell me more, how much time do we have? Is Dadaji very ill?" uttered Daksha. "No on the contrary your grandpa is really fine, no physical problems or pains as of now. I talked to one of my colleagues who is an oncologist, and told him about the reports. He said the tumor is small now but it would increase in size and cause pain. The way he suggested is to operate but it comes with a problem too" informed Rima. "Tell me everything clearly, please do not hide anything" said Daksha with the broken soul.

"Listen your Dadaji is seventy plus, operating at this age might lead to brain death or even death". "Is there no hope?" asked Daksha crying. ''See Daksha, at present there is no risk as the tumor is small, it would not cause harm for the time being but it is growing day by day and it would cause pain later then we will have to go for the operation. For the time being if you want, we may avoid the operation because he is really doing well without any pain or any physical problems. Now it's up to you to decide whether you would like to wait till he gets the pain or operate right away". ``Does Dadaji know about this?" asked Daksha. ``Grandpa is too intelligent to guess what's going on, and I could not lie to him when he demanded to know. I will get back to you later. Take care Daksha and be bold. Try to face the reality. Bye" exclaimed Rima.

It was four in the morning; sun would rise soon. The night passed in darkness and even the morning sun could not provide any hope to Daksha. She did not have any feelings of sleeplessness, tiredness or hunger. She felt lost amidst the concrete jungle. She wished to be a little Daksha again and run to her grandfather's lap but the situation did not permit her to show such emotions. Soon she had to get ready for the meeting. Huge responsibility on her head to get the deal for her company. She felt mentally exhausted. She somehow managed to dress well and presentable and pulled herself to the meeting destination. The meeting however went well. She couldn't wait to sign the deal and ran back to her hotel asking her company to book an urgent flight to India that evening. Return flight for that evening was not available, so Daksha had to wait for the next evening. She skipped her dinner that night. Had no drive for eating. She called up her grandfather to know how he was. To her amazement he sounded fit and happy. "Hi Dadaji, I am done with my work. I would board tomorrow and would reach by the day after tomorrow". ``You need not hurry dear; see I am absolutely fine. Do I sound low to you?" said her grandfather enthusiastically. "What did you eat for dinner Dadaji?" asked Daksha. "Oh, some rice and chicken, ordered from out. I feel lazy to cook only for myself. After you are back, I will cook your favourite dish." Silence was on both the sides till Daksha said in soft voice "Dadaji, I love you. Get well soon." "Love you too dear. Goodnight" replied Dadaji sounding like the old man mentally.

Daksha felt a bit better after talking to her grandfather. She changed her dress and went to bed. The silence of the room was broken by the ticking of the clock which reminded her of the passing time and the increasing tumor. She does not remember how long was she tossing in bed till she fell asleep.

"Thank you Dadaji", I love the cake, it's so yummy. Let's go and bake chicken in the garden. "Surely my dear, I know you love baked chicken. Let's make it together". They moved out into the garden with the needed spices and chicken. "I love all chicken prepared by you Dadaji".

"I know that dear but you should learn to cook as well. How will you manage when I will not be there anymore?"

"Dadaji never say such things. I will always be with you and you will always be with me. Always happy we two together" exclaimed Daksha with eyes filled. ''Daksha you are no more a kid now you need to understand a thing that no-one lives forever dear, so the same would happen to me. I am not an immortal beti."

Daksha turned to fetch the sauce with tears in her eyes. "You know Daksha one day I will return back to the sky from where I came and from where we all come." "Enough Dadaji, why do you need to say such things and make me cry?"

Daksha turned towards her grandfather and noticed him re

treating slowly into the dark woods behind her house. Daksha felt terrified and ran to stop her grandfather till she fell and wounded her elbow. She went on shouting till she woke up getting hurt in her elbow, found herself lying on the floor.

It was a bad dream, a nightmare. She was so traumatized with the news that it affected her subconscious mind producing such dreams. She checked her watch and it was 7am. She slept long due to physical tiredness but her mind was continuously hovering over her grandfather's condition. She woke up sweating profusely. She felt hungry. She found a pack of biscuits in her backpack which her 'Dadaji' had bought for her. She gulped them hungrily and thought of calling her grandfather. It was too early and decided not to disturb his sleep. She decided to have a hot bath to calm down her nerves. Few hours to wait before she would go to the airport. It was 11am. She moved down and ordered a light meal. She ate her food while talking to her grandfather. She decided to go shopping and to buy a nice gift for her grandfather. While searching for the perfect gift, she found a sweater which she bought for the upcoming winters. She kept strolling aimlessly in the market to distract her mind. She called up Rima asking about her grandfather's condition and whether she visited him.

Daksha boarded the plane and kept waiting patiently for the next evening when she would land and meet him. She had given strict orders to her grandfather to rest at home and not to come to the airport to pick her up. She landed in India the next evening. Hired a cab and reached her place. Rang the bell. The door was opened by her grandfather. He was an old man of 70 but looked more aged and sicker than he looked before. Mr. Roy, Daksha's grandfather always had the habit of eating healthy and working out every morning. So, he always looked much fitter than his age. He was always cheerful but seemed to have been bowed down by illness now.

"Welcome back Daksha!" said her grandfather. He was surprised to see how broken Daksha looked.''Hi Dadaji, how are you?" asked Daksha, hugging him tight. ``Yes dear, I am absolutely fine. Go inside, freshen up quickly. I have asked the cook to make your favorite baked chicken. We will have it in our favorite spot, in the garden." "Sure Dadaji, let me change, I will be there soon" said Daksha smiling. First time in the past three days she had a hearty smile. Spending time in the garden with her grandfather seemed to rejuvenate her childhood memories. She rushed up to her room, changed into her home dress, freshened up and ran down with the gift in her hand.

Daksha saw her grandfather arranging the plates and other things on the table, humming a song to himself. When Daksha was small, she would run to her grandpa and hug him from the back but she is grown up now and has to take a huge responsibility and decide about what step to take next. Earlier all her responsibilities were her grandfather's but now the situation is quite the reverse. She quietly stepped into the garden. Hearing the footsteps her grandfather looked behind.

"The chicken smells marvelous Dadaji" said Daksha, forcing a smile on her lips. "How was your meeting there? Did you get the deal?" asked her grandpa. "Yes! it was quite a success, Sir praised me a lot for this". Both the grandfather and the grand-daughter sat at the table, as usual her grandfather took the charge of serving. Earlier Daksha would have been thrilled to have an outdoor lunch with her Dadaji and especially her favorite baked chicken with lemon rice but the situation was such that her senses failed to respond to the hunger stimulating smell. She looked down at her plate while her grandfather served her and himself.

"Hey beti, try it quick or else it will turn cold". Daksha took one bite and found it to be as tasty as it used to be before. She looked at her grandfather; he too looked the same cheerful and happy in the company of Daksha. "You no Daksha, I used to make this for your mother too. She loved it just like you do. When she was ex-pecting you, it was our regular Sunday meal" said her grandfather recollecting his old memories. "Do you miss Mom, Dad and Dadi, Dadaji?" asked Daksha. "Well, she was my daughter and so I do miss her every day, every time, especially when we have an outdoor lunch or dinner. I miss them all beti" he replied being emotional.

"Dadaji, after my parents expired wasn't it difficult for you to take care of me?""Did you ever feel I had any problems taking care of you?" You were my good little girl Daksha. My all, only refuge and everything" said her grandpa smiling but emotion-al. Silent dominated the table except the noise of cutlery on the plates and pouring of water on the glasses. After dinner was over Daksha put the utensils in the dishwasher while her grandfather sat in the easy chair in the garden looking at the sky. Putting the dishes to wash, Daksha joined her grandfather. The sky looks pretty clear today. The cold breeze blowing shows winter would arrive soon. After some moments of silence Daksha asked him

"Dadaji did you feel sad when my parents died and left us?"

"Of course, I was sad, I'm still unhappy and broken, I felt lost as to what to do next...your parents were my only family, they were my children." "So, what did you do then?" asked Daksha. Mr. Roy said "I was very helpless Daksha; you were too small then and it was too difficult for me to cope up especially without your mom. Even your Dadi was not there with me then. One night I was sitting looking towards the sky, your cradle was beside me. You were fast asleep. I looked up in the sky recollecting the memories of those days when I and your Dadi, your parents used to spend sleepless nights chatting with each other with a cup of coffee in the garden. I missed them so much, tears ran down my cheeks. But I looked at the stars, the sky, and the moon. Everything around us, which portrayed their presence and reminded me that they existed and they would exist forever in my memories" replied her grandpa with a smile while looking at the stars. Suddenly he heard weeping sound and looked at Daksha who was weeping.

"What happened Daksha why are you weeping?" the question seemed to make her cry more. She hugged him and said "Dadaji, what am I to do without you? I have no-one apart from you in this whole world. How will I live alone?"

Daksha's grandfather looked at her affectionately, "why do you think I will go away leaving you alone? Didn't I just say you, your parents and Dadi are still there with me, even when they are not? Listen Daksha no-one is immortal, all has to go one day. Do u know what is immortal? The memories of the person in our heart till we ourselves live. When a person is alive, we seem to value them less but when one is dead one tends to miss him more and thereby love for him becomes intense. You need not think I will leave you and go. My dear just remember one thing I will always

be there in your heart and in your memories forever. Whenever you look at the sky, the moon, the stars, it will remind you of me."

Silence pervaded while the crickets crocked. "Daksha know one thing there is no point in being unhappy or to die every moment till the actual death comes. And beti, I have made death the reason to live more than I had ever lived."

21. The Wheel of Fortune

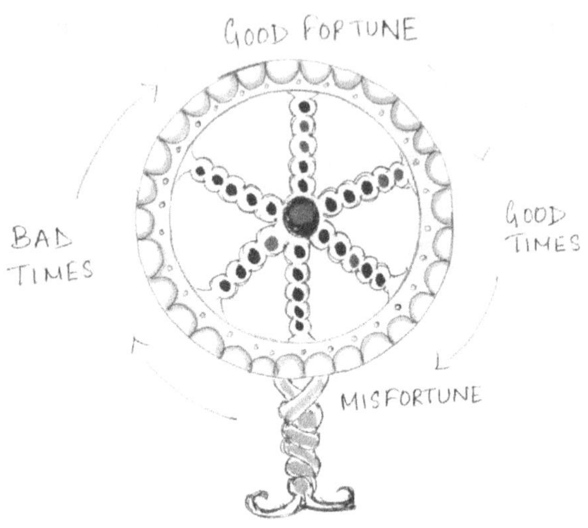

Whenever the things turn bad and messy,

Be sure that good times are near.

Whenever you feel hopeless,

Be sure that the future holds brightest hope for you.

Whenever you feel worthless,

Be sure something is about to happen to prove your worth.

Wherever there is darkness,

Be sure to find light at its end.

Change is the only constant thing in the entire Universe.

"Nothing is permanent" as taught by the preachers for centuries,
is the only truth.

The large wheel of fortune,

Always rotates, bringing changes,

Not only for those who bear its mood swings with a patient
heart,

But also, for those who doesn't.

22. The Eternal Truth

Look at the clock, its ticking away,

Do you know what that means?

With every ticking, a second, a minute and an hour,

A day, a month and a year is being reduced from your life.

You, who so ever you are, whatever is your name,

Wherever you stay whatever you do;

One day you will feel something escape your body

And going higher, escaping through the ceiling into the sky.

You realise it's you, suddenly you feel light as a feather,

You descend down and can see your lifeless body

Lying in bed as if in some deep unawakenable slumber.

You see your near and dear ones weeping and crying;

"Hello, why are you all crying? What has happened to me?

Can't you all hear me! Am I dreaming?"

You would scream and shout to make them hear you;

Until you realise that you have already crossed the realm of the
living,

And you do not belong here anymore.

You would not like to accept the reality,

And desperately try to touch and feel what is around you,

And try to connect with those who once belonged to you,

Until you realise they are far beyond your reach.

You will then see your body is being carried away,

To the cremation ground, and laying it on the pyre,

After Bathing and adorning it with new cloths and garlands.

No matter how badly you desire to return back,

There will be an invisible barrier holding you far from your
body.

Little by little you will see your carefully preserved body being
burnt to ashes;

The five elements will engulf your body!

While 'You', the eternal soul will get merged into the eternity-
the Cosmos.

You, whosoever you are, you no longer exist, in this realm of
the living.

Which, once you thought to be real and fought with your kith
and kin,

To establish your I-ness, your existence, your superiority.

Alas! The illusion of reality shattered, upsetting your long-cher-
ished dream,

Of maintaining your existence permanently in this world.

About Publisher

The publisher of the Solo book " Life- A Blooming Bud" authored by "Ms. Debalina Sarkar" is Power In Me Foundation. As the name suggest it is a Trust, that works on sustainable development model. It is established to work for the welfare of the people with rare diseases and their families. Publishing is one of the activities to help raise funds to carry out the activities aimed to creating awareness about various rare diseases, provide scholarships for studies, to provide for livelihood training, to provide for healthcare training, to establish centers for their care and various other objectives for social causes.

The authors associated with us follow the same vision to make the society a better place through their creative writing. We encourage raw talents with time to time guidance and exposure through our creative platform Ruh-E-Mohabbat by supporting and promoting them.

For any query on our publishing services, or supporting our cause to create awareness about rare diseases while empowering them you can reach us at mpowerinme@ gmail.com. You can even call/whatsapp at +91-8851537816.

Rare Diseases Awareness

Q. What Are Rare Diseases?

Ans. The diseases that have lower prevalence in the population are called rare diseases. They may be found in one in thousands to one in millions. About 95% of the rare diseases do not have any treatment available and only 5% have any treatment. The cost of treatment of these diseases is very high making it impossible for a normal family to afford it. Even the diagnosis of these diseases is difficult and takes approximately 5-6 years to identify right disease.

Q. How Do Rare Diseases Affect Mental Health?

Ans. There are some rare diseases that are directly affecting the mental health of an individual like Alzheimer, Bipolar, and Parkinson's Disease etc. because they affect the mind. However, majority of the rare diseases cause metal health issues because of the health conditions that arise and no treatment or very high cost of treatment. Families and patients face identity crisis, social discrimination, financial instability and often patients get accused with blames on misery in the family. This severely affects the state of mental health.